For Russell and Lisa,
my dear night people
—F.W.

To my family, Lesa, Jaime,
Maya, Malcolm, and Leila
—J.R.

It Is the Wind Text copyright © 2005 by Ferida Wolff Illustrations copyright © 2005 by James Ransome Manufactured in China by South China Printing Company Ltd. All rights reserved. www.harperchildrens.com Library of Congress Cataloging-in-Publication Data Wolff, Ferida. It is the wind / by Ferida Wolff ; illustrated by James Ransome. p. cm. Summary: At night various sounds lull a child to sleep. ISBN 0-06-028191-X — ISBN 0-06-028192-8 (lib. bdg.) [1. Sound—Fiction. 2. Bedtime—Fiction. 3. Sleep—Fiction. 4. Animals—Fiction.] I. Ransome, James, ill. II. Title. PZ7.W818554 It 2005 00-063197 [E]—dc21 CIP AC Typography by Elynn Cohen
1 2 3 4 5 6 7 8 9 10 ❖ First Edition

It Is the Wind

by Ferida Wolff
illustrated by James Ransome

HarperCollinsPublishers

What is the noise I hear,
in the night
that wakens me,
that shakens me,
the noise, I hear, in the dark
in the night?

It is the owl, I think,
on the branch
that whispers hooo,
that whispers booo,
the owl, I think, sitting high
on the branch.

It is the dog, I think,
in the yard
that's howling oooh,
that's howling wooooh,
the dog, I think, by the fence
in the yard.

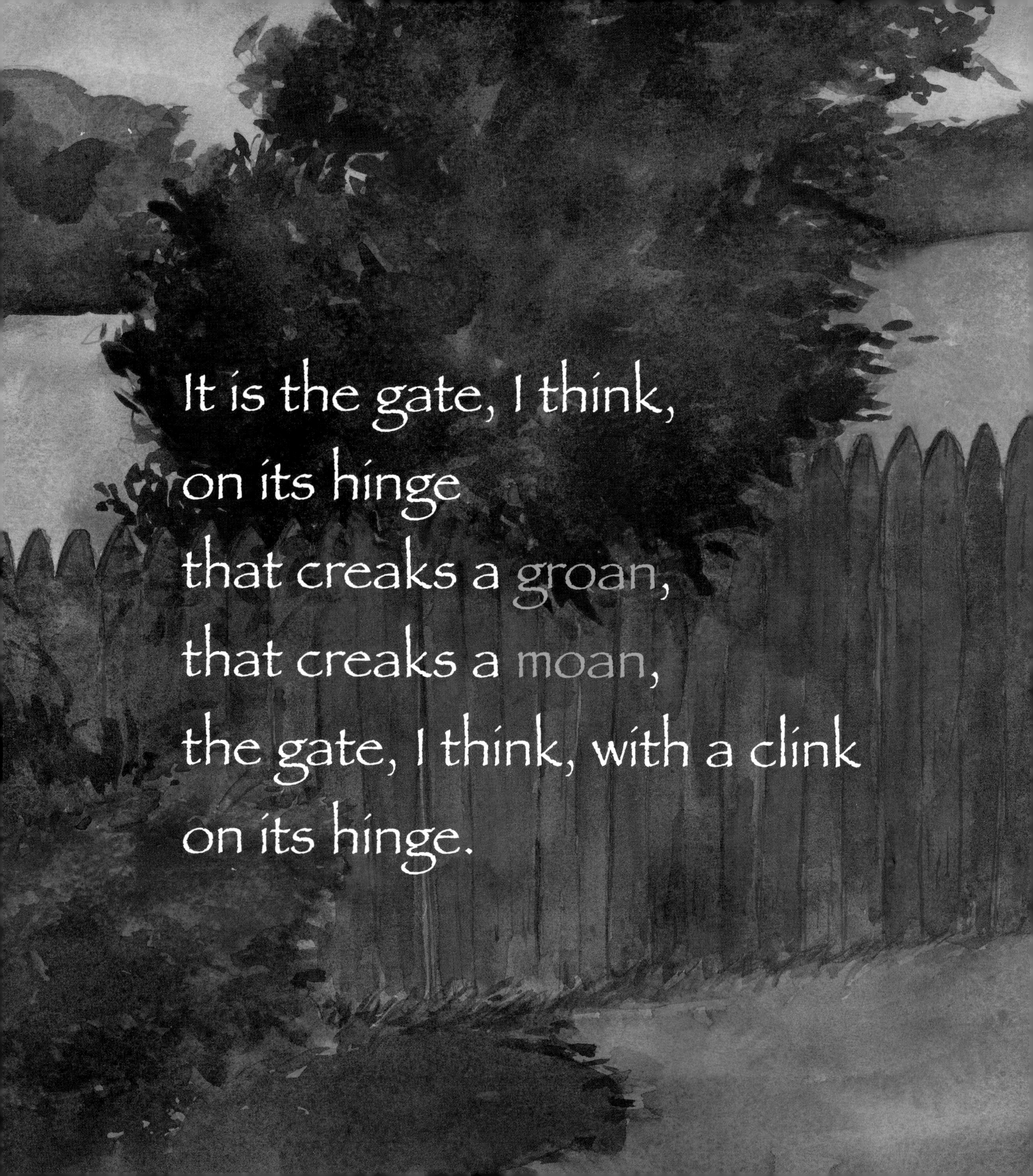

It is the gate, I think,
on its hinge
that creaks a groan,
that creaks a moan,
the gate, I think, with a clink
on its hinge.

It is the swing, I think,
by the barn
that sways and clunks,
that sways and thunks,
the swing, I think, in the breeze
by the barn.

It is the calf, I think,
on the loose
that calls out waaah,
that calls out maaah,
the calf, I think, down the path
on the loose.

It is the toad, I think,
in the pond
that makes the splash,
that makes the crash,
the toad, I think, on the log
in the pond.

It is the cat, I think,
in the woods
that hollers *yeeow*,
that hollers meeow,
the cat, I think, where it stalks
in the woods.

It is the hare, I think,
in the brush
that's pounding thump,
that's pounding bump,
the hare, I think, near the field
in the brush.

It is the bugs, I think,
in the grass
that stir and crick,
that stir and click,
the bugs, I think, singing songs
in the grass.

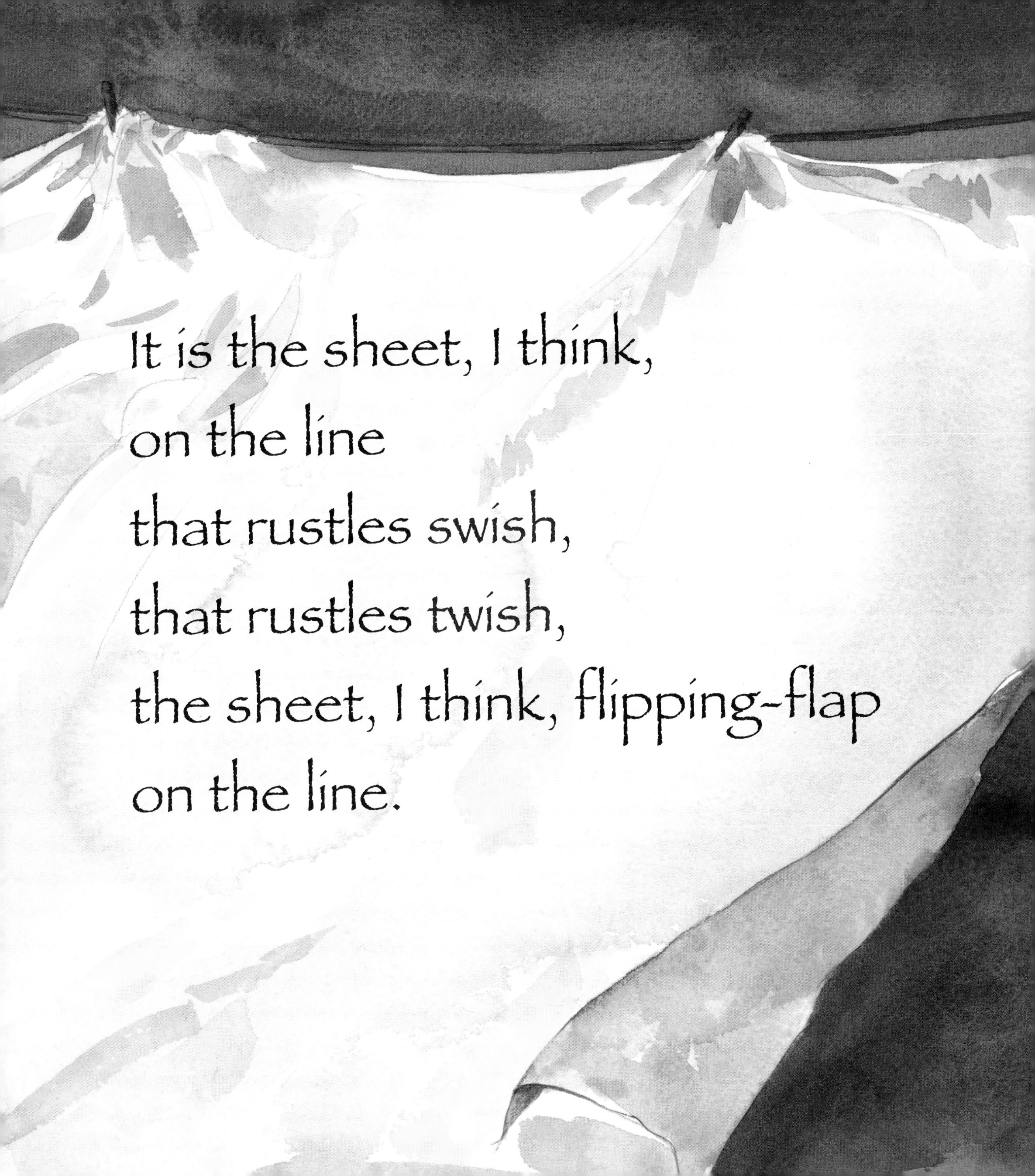

It is the sheet, I think,
on the line
that rustles swish,
that rustles twish,
the sheet, I think, flipping-flap
on the line.

It is the wind, I think,
that sighs, "Good night,"
that sighs, "Sleep tight,"
the wind, just the wind,
in the night
in my room.